The Frog Princess

and other princess stories

Compiled by Tig Thomas

Miles Kelly

First published in 2013 by Miles Kelly Publishing Ltd
Harding's Barn, Bardfield End Green, Thaxted, Essex, CM6 3PX, UK

2 4 6 8 10 9 7 5 3 1

Publishing Director Belinda Gallagher
Creative Director Jo Cowan
Editorial Director Rosie McGuire
Senior Editor Claire Philip
Senior Designer Joe Jones
Production Manager Elizabeth Collins
Reprographics Stephan Davis, Jennifer Hunt, Thom Allaway

ISBN 978-1-78209-220-9

Printed in China

British Library Cataloguing-in-Publication Data
A catalogue record for this book is available from the British Library

ACKNOWLEDGEMENTS
The publishers would like to thank the following artists who have contributed to this book:
Jennie Poh, Smiljana Coh, Mélanie Florian, Marcin Piwowarski, Helen Rowe (cover)

All other artwork from the Miles Kelly Artwork Bank

The publishers would like to thank the following sources for the use of their photographs:
Cover frame: Karina Bakalyan/Shutterstock.com
Inside frame: asmjp/Shutterstock.com

Made with paper from a sustainable forest
www.mileskelly.net   info@mileskelly.net

Contents

The Magic Key

By Howard Pyle

ONCE THERE WAS A PRINCE called John. One day his father said to him, "John, I am growing old, and I would very much like to see you married."

"Very well," said the prince, "and who shall I marry?"

"Why not the Princess of the White Mountain?" said the old king.

"Why not, indeed?" said the young prince, "only she is too short."

"Why not the Princess of the Blue Mountain?" said the old king.

"Why not, indeed?" said the young prince, "only she is too tall."

"Why not the Princess of the Red Mountain?" said the old king.

"Why not, indeed?" said the young prince, "only she is too pale."

"Then who will you marry?" said the old king in desperation.

"I do not know," said the young prince, "but her skin shall be as white as milk, her cheeks shall be as red as blood, her eyes shall be as blue as the skies, and her hair shall be like spun gold."

"Then go and find her!" said the king.

So the prince travelled on until his shoes were dusty and his clothes were grey.

Nothing was in his bag but a piece of brown bread and some cold meat. After a while he came to a crossroads, and there sat an old woman. She looked very sad.

"Please help me Sir, I am very hungry!" said the old woman.

The prince was a good-hearted fellow, so he said, "I only have a little food, but you are welcome to it." The old woman ate the prince's food as soon as he handed it to her.

"I am also very cold," said she.

"I only have this dusty coat, but you are welcome to it," said the prince.

"Thank you for your kindness," said the old woman, and she gave him an old rusty key. "If you look through the ring of it, you can see everything as it really is."

The prince wasn't sure what the old lady meant, but he travelled on, and at last he came to a castle that stood in the middle of a dark forest.

"I hope I shall find some food to

eat," said the prince, and he walked up the long path to the castle door, which he opened and went in. Only one person was within, and

that person was a maiden. She was covered in black soot from head to foot like a charcoal burner and dressed in filthy rags. The prince drew the rusty key out of his pocket and took a peep at her through its ring.

He saw that she was no longer dirty, but as beautiful as a ripe apple — for her skin was as white as milk, her cheeks were as red as blood, her eyes were as blue as the skies, and her hair was like spun gold.

"You are the one whom I seek," he said.

"Yes, I am," said she.

"And how can I free you from your enchantment?" the prince said.

"If you stay here three nights, and bear all that shall happen to you without a word, then I shall be free," said she.

"Oh yes, I will do that," said the prince. He had fallen in love at first sight.

After that the dirty princess set a supper before him, and the prince ate like a king.

A little while later there was a loud noise, the door opened, and in came an ugly troll with a head as big as a bucket. It rolled its great saucer eyes around till it saw the prince beside the fire.

"Black cats and spotted toads!" bellowed the troll. "Why are you here?"

But the prince never said a word.

The troll caught the prince by the hair and threw him around the room, but the prince never said a word. After a while the troll gave up and left.

The dirty princess found the prince tending his wounds and began to cry. When her tears fell on him his pain left him, and he was well again.

The next night the troll returned, and with him came two others. "Black cats and spotted toads!" bellowed the troll. "Are you here again?"

This time all three trolls flung the prince about, but he stayed quiet the whole time.

On the third night, the troll brought six others. The same thing happened as before, and they tried their best to make the prince make a sound. The poor prince was left very bruised, but he didn't say a word. He had fulfilled his task.

So, one last time, the princess came and wept over him, and before he knew it he was whole and sound again. The princess stood before him. Her skin was as white as milk, her cheeks were as red as blood, her eyes were as blue as the skies, and her hair was like spun gold.

Then the prince started his journey home, taking her with him. When they neared the palace the prince told the princess to wait for him nearby. He went and fetched her a dress of real silver and gold, such as was fitting for her to wear.

Then the happy couple rode into the town together where they were welcomed by all

The Magic Key

the people. The king was delighted that his son had found a bride at last and immediately ordered a grand wedding. The prince and the princess were overjoyed, and lived happily ever after for the rest of their days.

The Frog Princess

A traditional Russian tale

THERE WAS ONCE A KING who said to his three sons, "Let each of you shoot an arrow. The maiden who brings it back will be your bride." The eldest shot an arrow and a princess brought it back. The middle son let loose an arrow and a general's daughter brought it back. But Prince Ivan's arrow fell into a marsh and was brought back by a frog. The first two brothers were joyful but Prince Ivan was downcast. He wept, but there was nothing

for it, he had to marry
the frog. All three
couples were married on
the same day — the frog
being held up on a
silver tray.

Some time passed. One day the king wished to see which bride was the best at sewing. So he ordered them to make him a shirt. Poor Prince Ivan cried, "How can my frog sew a shirt? I'll be a laughing stock." The frog jumped across the floor croaking.

As soon as Prince Ivan was asleep the frog went outside, cast off her skin and turned into a beautiful maiden, calling, "Maids and matrons, sew me a shirt!" A host of servants appeared and brought a finely embroidered shirt. She took it and placed it beside Prince Ivan. Then she turned back into a frog as if nothing had happened.

In the morning Prince Ivan awoke and was overjoyed to find the shirt, which he took to the king. The king gazed at it and said, "Now there's a shirt for you, fit to wear on feast days!"

Then the middle brother brought a shirt, at which the king said, "This shirt is fit only for a cottage!" And taking the eldest brother's shirt, he said, "And this one is fit only for a smoky peasant hut!"

The king's sons went their separate ways, with the two eldest muttering among themselves, "We were surely wrong to mock at Prince Ivan's wife, she must be a cunning sorceress, not a frog."

Presently the king again issued another command. This time the two eldest son's wives were each to bake a loaf of bread, and bring it to him to judge which bride was the best cook. The other two brides had made fun of the frog, but now they sent a maid to see how she would bake her loaf. The frog noticed the woman, so she kneaded some dough, rolled it out and tipped it straight into the fire. The chambermaid ran to tell her mistresses, the royal brides, and they did the same.

But the crafty frog had tricked them. As soon as the woman had gone, she got the dough out, cast off her skin and called, "Maids and matrons, bake me a loaf of bread such as my dear father used to eat on Sundays and holidays." In an instant the maids and matrons brought the bread. She took it, placed it beside Prince Ivan, and turned into a frog again.

In the morning Prince Ivan awoke, took the loaf of bread and gave it to his father who looked at it and said, "Now this is bread fit to grace a holy day. It is not at all like the burnt offerings of my elder daughters-in-law!"

After that the king decided to hold a ball

to see which of his sons' wives was the best dancer. All the guests and daughters-in-law assembled. Everyone was there except Prince Ivan, who thought, 'How can I go to the ball with a frog?' The poor prince was very sad indeed. "Do not despair, Prince Ivan," said the frog. "Go to the ball. I shall follow in an hour." Prince Ivan was cheered at the frog's words, and left for the ball.

Then the frog cast off her skin and turned into a lovely maid dressed in finery. When she arrived at the ball, Prince

Ivan was overjoyed, and the guests clapped their hands at the sight of such beauty. When the ball was over, Prince Ivan rode off ahead of his wife, found the frogskin and burnt it. So when his wife returned and looked for the skin, it was nowhere to be seen. She said to her husband, "Oh, Prince Ivan, if only you had waited a little longer the spell I am under would have been broken and I, Yelena the Fair, would have been yours forever. Now God alone knows when we shall meet again. Farewell. If you wish to find me you must go beyond the Thrice-Nine Land to the Thrice-Ten Kingdom." And she vanished.

Prince Ivan set off to seek his princess. He came to a little hut, and cried, "Little hut turn your face to me, please, and your back to the trees." The little hut did as he said and Prince Ivan entered. There before him sat an old woman, who cried, "Fie, Foh! Where are you going, Prince Ivan?"

"I seek Yelena the Fair," he replied.

"Prince Ivan," the old woman said, "you've waited too long! She has begun to forget you and is to marry another. She is with my sister who will not wish her to return to you. Go there now, but beware — as you approach they will know it is you. Yelena will turn into a spindle, her dress will turn to gold. My sister will wind the gold thread around the spindle and put it into a box, which she will lock. You must find the key, open the box, and break the spindle. Then she will appear."

Off went Prince Ivan, and up he came to the old woman's hut. As he entered he saw her winding gold thread around a spindle.

She then locked it in a box and hid the key. But Prince Ivan quickly found the key, opened the box, took out the spindle and broke it as he had been told. All of a sudden, there was Yelena the Fair standing in front of him.

"Oh, Prince Ivan," she sighed, "how long you were in coming! I almost wed another." And Prince Ivan and Yelena the Fair went home and they lived happily ever after.

The Blacksmith's Daughter

Anon

IN A WOODEN HOUSE deep in the forest lived a blacksmith and his daughter. The blacksmith worked hard all day shoeing horses, while his daughter pumped up the fire, carried water from the well, chopped wood, dug the garden, picked fruit from the trees, trimmed the candles and cooked the meals. Her hands were rough and coarse, her face pale with work and little sleep, and her hair matted with dirt. Even so, some men came seeking her hand in marriage.

"What's the good of that?" said the girl, "I won't marry till I find someone I love with all my heart."

One day, the king's messenger came riding through the land to proclaim that the prince of the kingdom had been enchanted by a wicked sorcerer. He was imprisoned in a deep cave sealed with three locks. The king was offering a reward of the greatest treasure in his kingdom to anyone who could rescue the prince. All the young nobles of the land saddled their horses and went off to try their luck.

The next day, the blacksmith's daughter put down her tools and said, "Father, if you can get along without me, I've a mind to try and rescue the prince myself." She had seen a picture of the prince, and it pained her heart that anyone with such a merry face should lie under such an evil enchantment.

So she packed a bundle with some bread, clothes and her tools. She walked through the forest, day after day, sleeping where she could and earning a little money for food, till she came to the place of the enchantment. The king and queen were there, as was the king's messenger, who had proclaimed of the prince's capture.

There stood the greatest wonder she had ever seen — a cave with an iron door three feet thick, with three mighty keyholes. In front of the cave stood three huge pillars, towering into the sky, one of flame, one of ice, and one of wax.

"On the top of each pillar," explained the king's messenger, "is a key to one of the keyholes. But the wax pillar is too smooth to climb, the ice pillar too slippery, and the fire pillar has killed scores of our best knights."

All day the blacksmith's daughter watched as man after man tried their luck. They showed great courage and daring but the three pillars defeated them all. Many were badly hurt, and all were carried away to be tended in the king's tent, for the king and queen watched every attempt, praying for success to free their son.

At last it was the blacksmith's daughter's turn to try.

"Humph," she said. "This is work for

someone who understands work."

She went into the forest with her axe, gathered huge bundles of wood and built an enormous fire around the base of the ice pillar. Next she dug a channel between the ice pillar and the fire pillar. She lit the fire and with her bellows, puffed and puffed until she had a roaring blaze. Steadily, slowly, the ice began to melt. At first it dripped slowly but soon the water rained down in torrents, and the pillar dwindled and dwindled. As the ice melted, the water gathered in the channel she had dug and ran down to the pillar of flame. It surged against the pillar and the fires at the bottom died away with a hiss. The whole pillar slowly collapsed downwards.

As it fell, the key from the top of it shot into the grass where the blacksmith's daughter snatched it up. At the same moment, the ice pillar dwindled to a height where she could finally reach up to seize the key from its top.

Only the pillar of wax was left. She scooped up a great shovelful of hot coals from the pillar of flames, and spread them at the base of the pillar of wax.

The heat softened the wax just enough to allow her to carve out small holes, like steps, in its side. Putting her foot into the first hole and quickly cutting another one for her hand, she started to climb. Up she went, steadily cutting holes with her hand axe. When she reached the top, there lay the third key. She picked it up and climbed swiftly down, for the wax was becoming dangerously soft, and dripped around her.

As she slid to the ground, a cheer went up, and the king himself rose from his platform and came forward. The three keys were fitted to the locks and out came the prince.

His gaze fell on the blacksmith's daughter. The ice water had washed the dust and dirt from her hair, the fire had put colour in her cheeks and the wax had softened her hands. The prince could not take his eyes off her.

"You deserve any reward you care to claim, even to half my kingdom," said the king. "Name it and it shall be yours."

The blacksmith's daughter said simply,

"Your majesty offered as a reward his greatest treasure. Is not the prince himself your greatest treasure?"

"Do you mean?" asked the queen, but the eyes of the prince and the blacksmith's daughter had spoken without words, and each knew what the other wanted. The prince drew her to him, the king signalled his approval and the people gave a cheer. They knew one day the prince would be their king and it would be useful to have a queen who knew how things worked.

The Goose Girl

By the Brothers Grimm

A QUEEN HAD A BEAUTIFUL DAUGHTER, who was going to be married to a young prince of a neighbouring kingdom. It was arranged that she was to travel to his country accompanied by her maid. The queen provided the princess with many beautiful robes and jewels, and gave her a wonderful horse named Falada, which had the amazing gift of speech.

Just before the princess started on her journey, the queen pricked her finger, and dropped three drops of blood upon a handkerchief. "Take this my dear," she told her daughter. "It will serve you if you are ever in danger."

They shed many tears at parting, but at last the princess mounted Falada and started on the journey.

When she and the maid had ridden for some time, they came to a stream of clear water. The princess asked the

maid to bring her a drink of water, but the girl replied rudely that she could get the water for herself.

The princess dismounted and drank from the stream, but as she raised her head the handkerchief bearing the three drops of blood fell from her dress and floated down the stream. The maid noticed and was very pleased. Without the three drops of

blood, the princess was completely in her power, and the nasty servant immediately forced the princess to exchange her royal dress for her own servant's one.

After making her promise never to betray the terrible secret, the maid mounted Falada and left her own horse for the princess. Falada took the false princess to the palace, and when they arrived the prince came out to meet them, and took the false bride to the royal chamber. The true bride had followed on the maid's horse, and was left in the court below. Seeing her there, forlorn and beautiful, the king inquired who she was.

"Only my servant," the false bride carelessly replied. "Give her some work to keep her busy."

So the king sent the true princess to help a boy called Curdken herd geese — and so it happened that the real bride became a goose girl.

One day shortly after, the false bride remembered Falada's gift of speech and became worried he might give her away. She told the prince that the horse was vicious, and that she wished its head to be cut off. The prince, having no reason to doubt her, at once carried out her orders.

When the real princess heard the sad news, she dried her tears and sought the executioner. She could not save her dear Falada from his doom, but she persuaded him to place the horse's head over the great gate through which she had to pass on her way to the goose pasture.

The next morning, when she and Curdken drove their geese under the gate, the princess cried, "O Falada, hang you there?" And to

the princess's astonishment the horse head at
once replied to her,

   "'Tis Falada, Princess fair.

     If she knew this, for your sake

     Your mother's heart would break."

   When she had driven the geese to the
field, the princess sat down and let her
golden hair down.

   The sun shone upon it, and Curdken
caught at its golden threads and tried to pull
one out as a keepsake but the goose girl
called to the wind,

   "Wind, blow gently here, I pray,

     And take Curdken's hat away.

     Keep him chasing o'er the world,

     While I bind my hair of gold."

   The wind did as she asked, and Curdken
ran so far for his hat that when he returned
the golden hair was plaited and bound

about her head. Curdken was cross all day long, and when at night they had driven the geese home, he complained to the king.

"The goose girl so teases me that I will no longer herd the geese with her."

When asked how she had offended him, he told the king that she spoke every morning to the horse's head that was over the gate, and that the head replied and called her princess. When morning came the king arose early and stood in the shadow of the town gate. He heard the goose girl say, "O Falada, hang you there?" And he heard the head answer.

Then the king followed on to the field, where he hid behind a bush and watched them herd the geese.

After a time the goose girl undid her glittering hair, and as Curdken snatched at it, the king heard her call the wind again.

The wind came at her bidding, and carried the boy's hat across the fields while she combed her shining hair and fastened it in place.

The king quietly returned to the palace, and that night he sent for the goose girl. He told her he had watched her at the gate and in the field, and asked her the meaning of her strange actions.

"I may not tell, for I swore that if my life was spared I would speak to no one of my woes," she replied.

The king pleaded with her, but she was firm, and at last he told her to tell her troubles to the iron stove, since she would not confide in him. When he had left her, she fell upon her knees before the stove and poured forth her sorrows.

"Here am I, the daughter of a queen, doomed to be a goose girl, while the maid steals my treasures and my bridegroom."

She sobbed until the king, who had stood outside and heard all, came in and told her to dry her eyes. He ordered her to dress in royal robes, and she looked beautiful. The prince was summoned, and the old king told him the story. He showed the prince the true bride. He knelt at her feet in admiration, and knew her to be the real princess. When the wicked maid had been punished, the princess was married to the young prince, and reigned with him for many happy years over the kingdom where she had first served as a goose girl.